For Kim and Jimmy – M.D.

For Anna – A.W.

Molly and the Whale published by Graffeg in 2019.
Copyright © Graffeg Limited 2019.

Text copyright © Malachy Doyle, illustrations copyright
© Andrew Whitson, design and production Graffeg
Limited. This publication and content is protected by
copyright © 2019.

Malachy Doyle and Andrew Whitson are hereby
identified as the authors of this work in accordance with
section 77 of the Copyrights, Designs and Patents Act
1988.

A CIP Catalogue record for this book is available from the
British Library.

ISBN 9781913134044

Mali a'r Morfil (Welsh edition)
ISBN 9781913134327
Muireann agus an Míol Mór (Irish edition)
ISBN 9781912929030

1 2 3 4 5 6 7 8 9

MALACHY DOYLE   ANDREW WHITSON

MOLLY AND THE WHALE

THIS BOOK BELONGS TO

_____

_____

_____

GRAFFEG

Molly and Dylan went down to the shore the morning after the storm.

They were looking for crabs, or cowrie shells, or anything little and interesting that might have been washed up in the night.

But there, on the beach, was a whale.

'Daddy! Daddy!' yelled Molly. 'There's a great enormous whale on the beach! She must have come in on the storm, and the sea's gone out and left her behind!'

'Fetch the buckets and spades,' said her father.

'I'm not sure how making sandcastles will help,' muttered Molly, but she did as he asked.

'Right, children,' said Molly's dad. 'Fill the buckets with water and pour it over her. As it's low tide, we need to cool her down till the sea comes back in again.'

So Molly, Dylan and their friends made
sure the whale's skin didn't dry out.

And meanwhile Molly's father and the
others dug a trench all around, so the
water would keep her cool while the
tide rose.

9

'Oh, you poor thing!' said Molly to the whale.
'Can't we push her back into the sea, Dad?'

Her father shook his head. 'She's too heavy, love.
And anyway, we might hurt her. Hopefully, at
high tide, when the water comes back up the
beach, she'll be able to swim away.'

11

All afternoon, they dug and they poured.

And all the while Molly sang a little song to the whale,
to try and calm her.

'We're keeping you wet, through the heat of the day.
We're doing our best till you're safe and away.
As long as it takes, we'll be here by your side.
As long as it takes, till you swim on the tide.'

The whale seemed to like Molly's song. She seemed to like that people were trying to help her.

But Molly sensed that, as the day warmed up, the massive creature got more and more uncomfortable. More and more unhappy.

'We're keeping you wet, through the heat of the day,' Molly sang again.

'We're doing our best till you're safe and away.'

'High tide's coming!' cried Dylan, at last.

The children ran to the shoreline and dug a channel
to try and speed the water up.

At long last, the first wave reached the stranded whale.

The trench the grown-ups had dug began to fill up, so
that soon her tummy was resting in the cool clear water.

And the whale did a big blubbery shake, as if to say
thank you.

The tide kept coming.

'Will there be enough water for her to swim away, Dad?' asked Molly. 'She's so big and heavy!'

'I hope so,' said her father. 'I really hope so.'

By high tide everyone was up in the dunes, watching and waiting.

But the water still wasn't deep enough.

'She'll never get back to the sea!' cried Molly, fighting back her tears.

'The poor whale needs to be quiet now,' Molly's dad told everyone. 'You all go home and I'll wait with her. It's full moon tonight, so the next tide will be even higher. Hopefully then she'll be able to swim.'

So everyone else went off to bed. Everyone but
Molly and Dylan, who wouldn't leave. Night fell,
and by the light of the moon and stars, they
watched, they waited, and quietly they sang.

'As long as it takes, we'll be here by your side.
As long as it takes, till you swim on the tide.'

Molly woke.

The first light of morning was breaking through the clouds.

The tide was higher than before. And...

'Look!' she cried, waking the others. 'She's splashing her tail, to see if the water's deep enough to swim!'

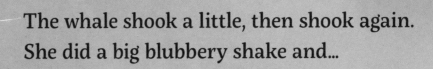

The whale shook a little, then shook again.
She did a big blubbery shake and...

'She's moving!' yelled Dylan.

'She's swimming! cried Molly. 'She's heading out to sea!'

And they watched in silence as the enormous creature swam off, into ever deeper, ever safer, water.

'Look!' cried Molly. 'She's happy again now!'

'She certainly is,' said her dad. 'And I think she's trying to say thank you...'

Dylan, Molly and her dad cheered, hugged and then trundled off home, singing Molly's song.

'We were keeping you wet, through the heat of the day.
Doing our best, till you're safe and away.
As long as it took, we were there by your side.
As long as it took till you swam on the tide.
Goodbye, whale! Goodbye!'

Malachy Doyle

Malachy Doyle grew up by the sea in Northern Ireland, and after living in Wales for many years has returned to Ireland. He and his wife Liz bought an old farmhouse on a little island off the coast of Donegal, where they live with their dogs, cats and ducks.

Malachy has had well over a hundred books published, from pop-up books for toddlers to gritty teenage novels. Over the years he has won many prestigious book awards, and his work is available in around thirty languages.

His recent books include *Rama and Sita, Jack and the Jungle* and *Big Bad Biteasaurus* (Bloomsbury), *Fug and the Thumps* (Firefly Press), *Cinderfella* (Walker Books) and *Ootch Cootch* (Graffeg), which is illustrated by his daughter, Hannah Doyle.

Andrew Whitson

Andrew has illustrated books on various aspects of Irish mythology including *The Creatures of Celtic Myth, The Field Guide to Irish Fairies* and *The Dark Spirit*.

Since 2007, he has illustrated a series of popular children's picture books: *Gaiscíoch na Beilte Uaine* (Bisto shortlist, Ibby Award and Réics Carló Award 2007); *Balor* (Réics Carló Award 2009); *An Gréasaí Bróg agus na Sióga* (Bisto & Réics Carló shortlists 2010, R.A.I. winner 2011); *Mac Rí Éireann* (Réics Carló Award, Bisto illustration winner and R.A.I. winner 2011); *Ó Chrann go Crann* (CBI shortlist, Réics Carló Award 2012 and R.A.I. award 2013); *Pop!* (Réics Carló shortlist 2014); *An tÉan Órga* (R.A.I. shortlist 2015). In 2011, Andrew received the Bisto honorary award for book illustration. In partnership with Caitríona Nic Sheáin, Andrew has co-written and illustrated three books of fiction for children, *Cogito, Pop!* and *Cúraille i gCeannas*.

Graffeg Children's Books

Ootch Cootch
Malachy Doyle, illustrations Hannah Doyle

The Animal Surprises series
Nicola Davies, illustrations Abbie Cameron
The Word Bird, Animal Surprises, Into the Blue, The Secret of the Egg

Shadows and Light series
Nicola Davies, illustrations by various
*The White Hare, Mother Cary's Butter Knife, Elias Martin, The Selkie's Mate,
Bee Boy and the Moonflowers, The Eel Question*

Perfect
Nicola Davies, illustrations Cathy Fisher

The Pond
Nicola Davies, illustrations Cathy Fisher

Celestine and the Hare series
Karin Celestine
*Small Finds a Home, Paper Boat for Panda, Honey for Tea, Catching Dreams,
A Small Song, Finding Your Place, Bertram Likes to Sew, Bert's Garden*

Through the Eyes of Me
Jon Roberts, illustrations Hannah Rounding

The Knight Who Took all Day
James Mayhew

Gaspard The Fox
Zeb Soanes, illustrations James Mayhew

How to Draw series
Nicola Davies, illustrations Abbie Cameron
*The Word Bird How to Draw, Animal Surprises How to Draw,
Into the Blue How to Draw*

Paradise Found
John Milton, illustrations Helen Elliott

Mouse & Mole series
Joyce Dunbar, illustrations James Mayhew
*Mouse & Mole, Happy Days for Mouse & Mole,
A Very Special Mouse & Mole, Mouse & Mole Have a Party*

www.graffeg.com